Meet the Beanie Boos

By Joan Emerson

SCHOLASTIC INC.

Published by Scholastic Inc., *Publishers since 1920.* SCHOLASTIC and associated logos are trademarks and/or registered trademarks of Scholastic Inc.

The publisher does not have any control over and does not assume any responsibility for author or third-party websites or their content.

ISBN 978-1-338-25621-5

10 9 8 7 6 5 4 3 2 1

18 19 20 21 22

Printed in the U.S.A.

40

First printing 2018

Book Design by Becky James

Welcome to the World of Beanie Boos!

The Beanie Boos' world is full of beauty, wonder, and even a little magic! Beanie Boos live all over the world—in the Fantastical Forest, on the Mystic Mountains, in the Iridescent Islands, and even in the Shimmering Sky.

Each bighearted Beanie Boo is unique, but they all have one thing in common: They love making new friends. These cute and cuddly creatures can't wait to meet you!

Rainbow

All About Rainbow

Personal Poem:
They call me Poofie because of my hair.
It has style and flair and it's the coolest to wear.
Likes: Sunshine, selfies, good hair days
Dislikes: Stormy weather, dark colors
Favorite Food: Confetti cake
Hobby: Styling
Motto: Be you. There's no one
else like you!
Birthday: November 10

Rainbow's multicolored hair is an absolute showstopper. In fact, other Boos often stop her at the park to take her picture. But Rainbow doesn't want to be famous when she grows up. She wants to be a hairstylist to the stars and make them look as good as she does!

Kipper

All About Kipper

Personal Poem:
My baby must stay close to home
Until she is old enough to safely roam!
Likes: Hopping, playing outside
Dislikes: Watching TV, sitting around
Favorite Food: Vegemite
Hobby: Skipping
Motto: Make good choices!
Birthday: January 28

Kipper is an awesome mother. She's always making up fun games for her baby to play. She thinks it's important her little one gets lots of exercise. They play hopscotch and double Dutch jump rope together. Kipper even invented a brand-new game called Skipper!

All About Butter

Personal Poem:
I don't talk, I only moo.
That's my way of saying "I love you."
Likes: Hugs, chickens, warm tea
Dislikes: Fast talkers
Favorite Drink: Chocolate milk
Hobby: Singing opera
Motto: Moooooooo!
Birthday: January 12

Butter loves to sing. She dreams of becoming the first opera singer to sing all in "moos." Butter practices *a lot*. Sometimes she wakes the whole barn in the middle of the night! But no worries, she sings a moo-a-by to lull the other Boos back to sleep.

Fantasia

All About Fantasia

Personal Poem:
Come close . . . I have a secret for you.
I wish your dreams and wishes come true.
Likes: Glitter, rainbows, fireworks
Dislikes: Rain, frowns
Favorite Food: Cotton candy
Hobby: Galloping through the trees
Motto: Dream big!
Birthday: May 8

Fantasia lives deep in the Fantastical Forest with her unicorn pals. There is nothing she can't do! She believes that if you can dream it, you can achieve it! When her friends get upset, they turn to Fantasia. She can always cheer them up with a smile, a song, or some great advice.

Gabby

All About Gabby

Personal Poem:
Let me be your very best friend.
Then our playtime will never end.
Likes: Running, playing, talking to her friends
Dislikes: Alone time, sleeping
Favorite Food: Mozzarella sticks
Hobby: Playing hide-and-Boo-seek
Motto: Two heads are
better than one!
Birthday: June 2

Gabby loves to stay up late playing farm games with her friends. When her mom calls her home at the end of the night, she begs for a few more minutes to play. Her favorite game is hide-and-Boo seek. She is the farm champion! She keeps her trophy in her little barn bedroom.

Owlette

All About Owlette

Personal Poem:
Tuck me in to sleep at night,
But when you hug me, hold me tight.
Likes: Napping, cuddling, curling up with a good book
Dislikes: Bright lights, summertime
Favorite Drink: Hoot chocolate
Hobby: Reading
Motto: Keep calm and read on!
Birthday: April 20

Owlette always has his beak in a book. He lives in a tree house where his room looks like a giant library. If he doesn't know the answer to a question, he knows exactly which book will help him find it. He loves to share fun facts with his feathered friends.

Piggley

All About Piggley

Personal Poem:
I like to roll, hop, and play,
When all my friends jump in the hay!
Likes: Order, organization, bow ties
Dislikes: Messiness, confusion
Favorite Food: Broccoli
Hobby: Coloring in the lines
Motto: Less mess, less stress!
Birthday: March 8

Piggley might be a pig, but he likes everything very neat. When his friends splash in mud and puddles, Piggley stays far away. He likes to play by himself far from where things get messy. He loves tidying up and putting things away.

Kiki

All About Kiki

Personal Poem:
My friends call me kitty, kitty
Because they say I'm pretty pretty.
Likes: The color pink, bows, photography
Dislikes: Poor lighting, bad angles
Favorite Food: Spinach
Hobby: Modeling
Motto: Vogue! Strike a pose!
Birthday: August 16

Kiki dreams of becoming a world-famous model. She practices her strut every day on the kittywalk and poses in the mirror. She doesn't just want to be in front of the camera, she wants to be behind it, too. She loves photography and is always snapping great pictures of her friends!

Dotty

All About Dotty

Personal Poem:
If you stare at my bold, colored spots,
They might start to look like big crazy dots!
Likes: Music, tutus, and being on stage
Dislikes: Blending in, naptime
Favorite Food: Banana
chocolate-chip pancakes
Hobby: Dancing, of course!
Motto: It's better to
stand out than fit in.
Birthday: June 16

Dotty's colorful spots make her a one-of-a-kind leopard. Lucky for her, she loves to stand out. When Dotty grows up, she wants to be a famous ballerina. She's known for her signature twirl, the Dizzy Dot.

Slush

All About Slush

Personal Poem:
Through wind or sleet or rain or snow,
I'll take you where you want to go!
Likes: Cold weather, competition,
helping others
Dislikes: Hot days, sitting around
Favorite Food: S'mores
Hobby: Snowboarding
Motto: If you believe,
you can achieve!
Birthday: April 30

Slush is a seriously strong dog, and he's helpful, too! He leads a giant sled that takes everyone where they want to go. He loves snow sports and is training for the Beanie Boolympics!

Harriet

All About Harriet

Personal Poem:
I'm very important and my name is Harriet,
Because my special job is to lead the chariot!
Likes: Being on a team, cheerleading
Dislikes: Big hills, complaining
Favorite Food: Carrots
Hobby: Galloping
Motto: You can do it!
Birthday: December 20

Harriet has a seriously important job. She leads her chariot and encourages the other horses. It can be tough, but Harriet doesn't mind. She keeps the rest of the horses focused by calling out cheers. She knows hard work pays off.

George

All About George

Personal Poem:
I get excited when my friends visit me.
We talk and eat fruit while we sip our tea.
Likes: Bananas, talking, eating
Dislikes: Quiet, vegetables
Favorite Food: Green tea cupcakes
Hobby: Chatting with his chums
Motto: You can tell me anything!
Birthday: October 18

George loves to hang out with his friends and talk about everything that's happening in the forest. He doesn't like to call it gossip, though. He just happens to know everything that's going on. Maybe that's because he swings from tree to tree and helps others with their problems.

Gilbert

All About Gilbert

Personal Poem:
I like to lick peanut butter off a spoon.
But my mouth gets real sticky so I can't sing a tune.
Likes: Playing sports, making new friends
Dislikes: Short branches, unfair refs
Favorite Food: Peanut butter
Hobby: Volleyball
Motto: Why blend in when you
can stand out?
Birthday: August 23

With tall legs and a very long neck, Gilbert was born to stick out. Everyone across the plains knows him. He's fun and friendly and a terrific athlete. He can play almost any sport, but he's a total MVP in volleyball. Everyone wants him on their team.

Flippy

All About Flippy

Personal Poem:
I have big fins and I'm really cool.
They really sparkle when I'm in the pool!
Likes: Swimming, bubbles, school
Dislikes: Small spaces, rocks
Favorite Food: Seaweed chips
Hobby: Diving!
Motto: Dive in headfirst!
Birthday: January 3

Flippy is the best high diver in her school. She can flip forward and backward. She's best known for her Fliptastic Flip, where she whirls and twirls three times before entering the pool. When she glides through the water, the show doesn't stop!

Zippy

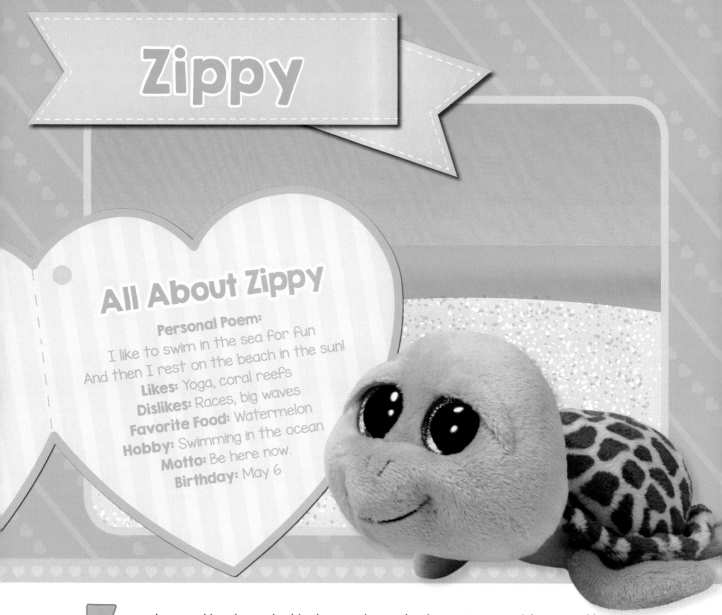

All About Zippy

Personal Poem:
I like to swim in the sea for fun
And then I rest on the beach in the sun!
Likes: Yoga, coral reefs
Dislikes: Races, big waves
Favorite Food: Watermelon
Hobby: Swimming in the ocean
Motto: Be here now.
Birthday: May 6

Zippy loves the beach. He loves to splash, swim, and lay on the rocks. He could spend all day by himself, soaring through the water. He thinks moving slow is better than being fast. After all, there's so much you miss when you go too quick!

Ellie

All About Ellie

Personal Poem:
When I stomp across the ground,
It always makes a great big sound!
Likes: Music, dancing, teamwork
Dislikes: Silence, naptime
Favorite Food: Squash
Hobby: Stomping
Motto: Live out loud!
Birthday: August 27

Ellie loves to move to the music. She's on her neighborhood's stomp team. They clap and stomp their feet to the rhythm of a drumbeat. Sometimes, Ellie gets a special solo where she stomps all by herself. Everyone says her feet make the loudest sounds. Afterward, the other elephants roar with applause.

Cinder

All About Cinder

Personal Poem:
Let's be friends and you will see,
I'm happiest when you are with me!
Likes: Fancy grills, parties, hanging
with friends
Dislikes: Quiet nights in, vegetables
Favorite Food: Hot dogs
Hobby: Grilling
Motto: It's party time!
Birthday: October 2

Cinder lives in a giant cave in the Fantastical Forest. She spends her mornings flying above the treetops. At night, she loves to be with her friends. She's a great host who's known for her flame-grilled barbecues!

Izzy

All About Izzy

Personal Poem:
Helping flowers grow is my biggest duty.
They get real big and show off their beauty.
Likes: Flowers, plants, working hard
Dislikes: Lazy days, climate change
Favorite Food: Raspberries
Hobby: Gardening
Motto: Save the Earth!
Birthday: July 18

Izzy lives in Friendly Field with tons of beautiful plants and flowers. She is very busy. She uses her ladybug watering can to feed the flowers. She makes sure they get plenty of water and lots of sunshine. In exchange, they let her live among them, giving her shade and protection.

Pixy

All About Pixy

Personal Poem:
At carnivals, I ride the Ferris wheel,
Then play some games and eat a meal!
Likes: Carnivals, prizes
Dislikes: Hiking, getting dirty, attention
Favorite Food: Funnel cakes
Hobby: Playing dress-up
Motto: I'm just me and that's good enough!
Birthday: May 26

Pixy is known throughout the Fantastical Forest for her incredible horn. Sometimes it looks rainbow-colored, sometimes it looks gold, but it's always beautiful. She's famous for it. If there's a big event like a carnival, Pixy would rather go unnoticed. So she dresses up in wacky disguises to fool everyone.

Wynnie

All About Wynnie

Personal Poem:
I relax in places where it is hot.
Let's be friends! Why not?
Likes: Sunshine, ocean breezes,
beach games
Dislikes: Rain, long flights
Favorite Food: Frozen drinks
Hobby: Doing the limbo
Motto: Relax! It's island time.
Birthday: September 19

Wynnie lives on the Iridescent Islands. Though he has beautiful wings, he would rather spend his time at a beach party than flying. He's the first one to start a conga line or challenge friends to a round of limbo. But sometimes he forgets the rules and flies right over the limbo stick!

Mandy

All About Mandy

Personal Poem:
My favorite time to have lots of fun
Is when I can run and play in the sun.
Likes: Cloud-watching, swimming
Dislikes: Sudden rainstorms, gossip
Favorite Food: Blueberries
Hobby: Making friends
Motto: It's what's inside
that counts!
Birthday: March 8

Mandy is famous for her blue fur. There's no other poodle that's quite like her! She adores the color blue, so she loves the way she looks. She even collects anything with blue in the title, like bluebell flowers and blues records. She is proud of the many shades of blue among her treasures.